Stay Out of the Woods

by Michael Elliott

DORRANCE
PUBLISHING CO
EST. 1920
PITTSBURGH, PENNSYLVANIA 15238

Dorrance Publishing Co
585 Alpha Drive
Suite 103
Pittsburgh, PA 15238
Visit our website at *www.dorrancebookstore.com*

ISBN: 979-8-88925-383-9
eISBN: 979-8-88925-883-4

Summary

After serving seven years in the military and being away from his friends, Chris, aka G.I. Chris, wants to have a camping trip at Fort Peck Lake in Montana to catch up and have a good time. To have his five friends together again and just enjoy life with one another. What they didn't realize was going on this trip means this could be the last time they ever see each other again...

Characters

1.) **Chris Johnson** -aka **G.I. Chris** - 27 years old- served seven years in the Army did two tours one in Iraq and one in Afghanistan getting out as a Staff Sergeant. (African-American)

2.) **Lisa Marsh**- 25 years old- teacher at Black Top Elementary School for the past three years (Caucasian)

3.) **Jamal Henderson**- 28 years old- history teacher and football coach at Lewis Jones High School- coach for Lockley Stacey High School for three years (African-American and Caucasian)

4.) **Patty Mill**- 26 years old- CEO of Baby Stay Dry and Comfortable Pampers (Native American)

5.) **Tracey Gilbert**- aka **Ms. Fix it**- 24 years old – automotive mechanic (Asian-American

6.) **Luis Jones**- aka **LJ**- 29 years old – regional manager of Get You In The Car Motors (Hispanic)

Extras

Park Ranger - Elliott

Park Ranger - Stacey

Park Ranger Dog- Lucky

Helicopter Pilot - Bruce

News Anchor - Katy Bonds

CHAPTER 1
THE DREAM

Chris Johnson: RUUUUUUUUN!

Gun fire goes off

Don't look back, keep running!

Wolves howling in the background

KEEP RUNNING, GUYS, DO NOT STOP!

Wolves howl and get closer to Chris. Chris falls and turns around to see a wolf swinging his claw to paint the ground with Chris's blood, he wakes up right before contact was made, Chris jumps up from out of his sleep. Heavy breathing. Cold sweat coming down Chris's face

Just another nightmare… just another dream.

Takes a deep breath and stretches an then rolls out of bed

Alright, time to get up and finish packing before everyone gets here. What can that dream mean?

Phone rings and rings and rings. Chris picks the phone up

Chris: Hello?

Jamal: Hey man, what's up? Are you ready for this weekend?

Chris: Yeah man, it's going to be fun! Should I bring some drinks?! Might as well get lit and have some real fun and not just sing campfire songs or tell scary stories. We're not kids anymore, hahaha.

Jamal: You already know G.I. Chris. Just get beer though okay, man, because that hard liquor makes people want to either argue or fight and wonder off and if they get lost it'll be hard to find them.

Chris: Yeah, yeah, I got it. See you soon. I have to finish some things up before LJ and Lisa get her.

Jamal: Okay, man, see you in a couple hours man. Peace.

Chris: Peace.

Chris: *Puts phone back into his pocket and heads to basement*

Alright, I got the tent, canned food, lighter fluid, matches, and extra water. Now the real question, which guns should I take? Should I take the .45 or 9mm hmm maybe the 9mm will not have a lot of kick back like the .45, but the .45 will scare off a predator if hit, I guess we'll go with the 9mm with hollow points and three extra mags. Now let us talk about ARs, we have the AR-15 or the AR-10 but maybe we can bring the AR-18 hmmm you know what we'll just take the AR-15. What time is it?

Pulls phone out

Okay its 3:44 P.M.

Puts phone away

Damn where the hell does the time go when picking up guns to take with you to go camping…

***Ding. Pulls phone back out.**

Group Chat- Squad

Lisa: Heyyyyyyy G.I. Chris what's your address again I lost it.

Chris: Yeah the address is 1719 S Black ave., Bozeman, Mt 59715. And It's a 5 hour drive up north so be ready.

Jamal: Bruuuuuuuuuh I hate you so much right now

Chris: I love you too ;)

Tracey: Can you guys take your bromance somewhere else? Some of us still have to pack and load up but can't do that with my phone going off lol.

Jamal: Awwww you want a hug Ms. fix it *eyes emoji*

Tracey: No... no I don't, well I do but not from you lol Patty: I'll hug her … :)

LJ: on my way to your G.I. Chris!

Chris: Ok man see you soon. If anyone comes tonight just text me and I'll let ya in. see ya soon whether tonight or tomorrow.

LJ: Bet

Lisa: On my way

Jamal: Alright i'm going to slide in the morning

Tracey: Yeah, what Jamal said I'm coming in the am

Patty: Ummmmm I'll probably come tonight so I don't have to leave early. See you later Chris.

Chris: Okay.

Chris yawns & checks phone

Chris- 4:23 Okay, let me take a nap before LJ always wants to drink ass.

Puts phone on charger and lays down

Lisa: Oh my God, oh my God, oh my God!

Heavy breathing

Chris, WHAT THE FUCK IS THAT THING?!?!? And Tracey, oh my God, what are we going to say to her parents?!?!?

Chris: Lisa, I don't know, but listen we need to stay quiet and we need to find the others! That fucking thing is fast!

Lisa: I saw you shoot it, and it didn't die. Why didn't it die?!?!?

Chris: I don't know but…

Lisa and Chris hear feet heading towards them.

If I am going to die tonight, I'm going out shooting!

Lisa: *Tears are running down her face mixing in with the blood that splattered on her from when the beast bite Tracey*

Oh God! Oh God!

Chris raises is 9mm in that direction ready to turn whatever comes through the bushes into a basket with holes in it

Bushes wrestling & footsteps coming closer

Jamal runs into Chris &=and Lisa where they're hiding. Chris is ready to grab his gun but doesn't pull the trigger realizing it's Jamal

Chris: Holy shit, Jamal I almost shot you!

Jamal: Bruh, what was that thing and where did it come from?!?! Have you seen the others?

Chris: No, Tracey, Lisa, and I ran away like everyone else and it chased us…

Jamal: Okay, so I see you and Lisa, where is Tracey?

Chris: …

Jamal: Where is she?!?!

***Tears started forming in Jamal's eyes, as if he already knew the answer by the way Chris and Lisa hung their heads below their**

shoulders. Lisa started crying again and now Jamal joined her in a heart-breaking moment. And that's when Lisa said…*

Lisa: It killed her… While we were running it grabbed her leg and tripped her and then pulled her back. I grabbed her hand trying to get her up to run again but as she was getting up it bit her neck and killed her… I tried to save her…

Jamal: You're lying, she can't be dead… she can't be dead, we were supposed to pick up things where we left off.

***Jamal is crying and Lisa goes to hold him but he pushes her away from him* Jamal**: Chris, you got your guns why didn't you shoot the damn thing?!?!?

Chris: I did! And I only have my pistol. The AR is in the truck still.

Jamal: Obviously you didn't, because if you did it wouldn't have killed it! Mr. Perfect Shot…

Lisa: He did… He did shoot it, it acted like the bullet didn't faze him and continued eating and tearing her apart…

Jamal: So you mean to tell me THAT THING GOT HIT POINT BLANK RANGE AND IT DIDN'T EVEN FLINCH?!?!

Chris: The pistol should've hurt it or something. But yeah, the bullets hit and we saw blood come out but it just tore Tracey apart and when we saw it unbothered we came here in these bushes to hide.

Jamal: Bruh, why the fuck is this even happening to us…

Jamal starts tearing up again thinking about Tracey and figuring out how the rest of them are going to get home when they hear…

Patty: *screams*

Chris: Okay, okay. Patty is still alive, but if those wolves are chasing her we don't know how much longer… We need to find her and try to get the others and run away or kill that wolf chasing her.

Lisa: But the last one you shot, do you think it's the one going after Patty!?!?

Chris: I don't know but …

Chris is interrupted by Patty's screaming.

Patty: HELP ME! PLEASE! SOMEONE HELP ME! *Screams*

LJ: This way over here! Listen, Chris and Lisa, when Patty comes through those bushes you grab Lisa out the way and Chris you put everything you have into that wolf's head, got it! PATTY OVER HERE!

They hear more screaming and sticks breaking as Patty get closer.

Chris: I don't know, but I am not going to let more friends die. I rather go out shooting than running and screaming! Got it!

Lisa: Got it!

As Lisa busts through the bushes right behind, Lisa grabs Patty pulling her to the left giving Chris a clean shot to the beast's face!

Chris: Take this, you stupid bitch!

Gun shots, gun shots, gun shots, ding dong, ding dong, ding dong

Chris wakes up from his nap drenched in cold sweat and realizes he was dreaming and that someone is at his house. He looks at his phone at 9:23 pm.

Who is at the door right now?

Beat being made on the door and Chris realizes who it is

Fucking Jamal, I'm coming I'm coming stop banging on my door before I whoop your tall going bald ugly ass.

LJ: Yo momma, come on man. Lisa and I have been out here waiting, bro, and I have to use the bathroom and she's hungry.

Chris: Lisa is here??

Goes to open the door, and as Chris opens the door all he sees is a mouth full of teeth

Ahhhhhhhh

*** Ding dong and phones ringing. LJ is calling***

Clears throat

Chris: Hello?

LJ: Bruh, we've been out here for three hours calling your phone. You good? Can you come open the door?!

Chris: Yeah man, be right there!

Gets up and starts to head to the door. Stops and goes back and grabs a 9mm and loads the gun

That thing isn't going to get me this time.

Opens door and put gun in LJ's face

LJ: OH SHIT! BRO, WHAT THE FUCK!

Chris: Oh damn, bro, my bad!

Puts gun down

Lisa: Are you okay?

Chris: *Clears throat*

Yeah, I'll explain in a minute, um, come on in.

LJ and Lisa walk into Chris' house. Chris closes the door and locks it. Everyone sits at the kitchen table

LJ: Soooo, you want to tell Lisa and I why I was about to see the big man in the sky?

Lisa: Yeah, Chris, what's up? Is someone after you or something? Is it PTSD?

Chris: What? No, it's not PTSD, and no one is after me. At least I don't think. Well now that you mention it there was that one old lady at the supermarket, but hey I saw that spot first and was faster but… ***sigh*** …I've been having these nightmares about werewolves attacking us on our trip, but I heard more of them in the distance. And we… we lost Tracey…

LJ: Damn… but why did you pull the gun on me?

Lisa: Yeah, that's just weird, we're not in the woods.

Chris: Because I had one of those *oh I'm awake but still sleeping* moments when the doorbell in my dream rang, I went to open the door like I just did and the wolf was there with an open mouth about to kill me and then I woke up to my phone… So better safe than sorry I guess my bad man.

LJ: You know that was just a dream, right? There's no such thing as werewolves.

Lisa: So do you want to cancel the camping trip?

LJ: No, we're not canceling this trip after all the driving I did, just bring the gun you were about to feed me and feed it to the supposed wolf. Besides, I kind of missed you guys…

Chris: See but I…

Lisa: We all drove, some long, some short, but Chris is home for good now. And Chris we'll be safe with you around and plus it was just a dream…

Chris: Alright, do you think I should tell the others?

LJ: I mean if you want to, but I wouldn't. I don't want to be that guy to spook everyone and be the cause of why we didn't have a good time.

Lisa: I am fifty-fifty on the situation. I don't want to ruin everyone's time, but I always feel like if you're having dreams like this maybe you should say something you know. Might be a representation of something else but not werewolves you know.

LJ: Lisa, let's just say we told them, then what? I mean it's just a dream on top of that what attacked us in your dream Chris, what was it again ah... ***snaps fingers*** Ah...

Chris: Werewolf

LJ: Bro, you know those aren't real right? I can't even remember the last time they even made a werewolf movie that was good but you two are thinking about calling off the camping trip because of a creature that doesn't exist and Chris you have more firepower to put one down. If they're real!

Chris: You make a strong argument and it's... ***checks watch*** ...almost 11:34 P.M. Well let's say we get some sleep, wake up early, load up my truck, and wait for the last three so we can head out on time sounds good?

Lisa: Okay.

LJ: Bet.

Chapter 2
The Morning

9:23 A.M.

LJ: *yawns, looks at phone to see the time*

9:23 A.M., bruh. Why is it so early?

sniffs air

Man, I'm not use to this smell time to wake up and bake my mind.

reaches for bookbag and pulls out a backwoods wrap

Now where is that lighter?

Someone walking upstairs

Chris: *knocks on LJ's door*

Yo, bro, we got food downstairs, and everyone is here and waiting on yo ass to get up and eat so we can head out. So stop beating your meat like it stole something, get dressed and let's go. We got a bit of a drive ahead of us.

LJ: *silence*

Kiss... my... ass... I'll beat my danger noodle if I want all over your soft cozy blan...

And before LJ could finish his sentence the door burst open with everyone rushing LJ

LJ: Aye yo what cha doing?!?!?

Chris: I got his legs!

Lisa: I'll grab his blanket!

Jamal: I'll hold his arms!

Tracey: I'll tickle him!

Patty: Standing in the doorway watching and laughing.

As LJ heard and saw them coming in, he beat them all to the punch and yells

LJ: I am naked!

They all froze… curious if they should try to call his bluff.

Chris: Bullshit!

charges him

LJ: ***Jumps on top of the bed like a spider monkey and throws the blanket at them and yells***

Look upon my anaconda!

Everyone but Chris: Ew dude, what the hell?

Chris: *being pro-military he is used to these kind of jokes and things*

Anaconda, more like a baby garden snake. Put some clothes on so we can hit the road.

Laughter fills the room

Jamal: Damn, you didn't have to do him like that, hahahaha.

LJ: Shut up, it's so cold in this room. That's why it's small right now, I'm a grower not a shower. Ask yo momma, Chris.

Silence…

Chris: I did, she told me she kept asking was it in yet.

Tracey: Damn, that backfired bad, didn't it LJ? Hahahaha.

Everyone heads out the room laughing and heads back downstairs with Patty still laughing. She looks to make sure everyone went downstairs.

Patty: Hey Mr. Danger Noodle, how have you been?

LJ: I've been good until ya tried jumping me and doing God knows what?

Patty: *chuckles*

Hey ,that was their idea, I just came to watch.

LJ: Hey, Patty…

Patty: Yeah, Luis…

Patty was the only one to call LJ Luis, for that matter the only one to ever know his real name. Luis never told anyone his real whole name. They always made guesses but never got them right except for the one night in college in a dorm room with Patty.

LJ: Do you…

Clears throat. You'd think LJ was in second grade and talking to his crush for the first asking if he can hold her hand

Do you umm… Do you… Do you miss me?

LJ is still laying in bed looking into Patty's light brown eyes waiting for her answer.

Patty: I… I…

She stutters

Boy, you sure don't wait, do you?

LJ: No, I don't you know this, but are you going to answer the question?

Patty: I, um... I got to go

Patty walks towards the steps and heads downstairs

LJ: Patty, wait… shit! She's gone.

exhales deeply

It's been years and she still makes my heart race faster than a 1,000cc motorcycle on an open road with no cops in sight.

Gets up out of bed and begins to put his clothes on

Does she still remember those late nights we spent together on the phone and long walks together until 4 A.M.? Man, I miss her.

Chris: *Yells*

LJ COME ON MAN!

Jamal: Aye, what if he's choking that chicken…

Tracey: One, that's weird, and two, LJ is many things but that nasty I doubt it.

LJ: Thank you, Tracey. Jamal, you're just mad.

Jamal: Mad at what?

LJ: Hmmm, you pick a reason and run with it, haha.

Chris: Anyway, ya both mad and ugly so there boom double struggle.

The attention turns to Chris now

LJ: I know your "oh my god she looked at me I am going to marry her" army ass isn't talking.

Jamal: This ole keeping dip companies in business ass, twenty-seven years old but knees and back act like he's seventy-seven years old and can hardly stand up, bum ass isn't talking.

Patty: Damn, ya going to tag team him like that though.

Lisa: Hahahahaha aye yooo hahaha.

Tracey: Now say sorry before…

Chris: *Interrupts Tracey*

Oh nah, Tracey, they don't have to say sorry, it's okay, because LJ ass couldn't get a woman to stay with him because he can't take things seriously and beats his dick harder than a Usman beat Covington the first time.

Lisa: Damn, and that man broke his face, hahahahaha.

Tracey: Dammmmmmmn, Jamal. Hahahaha.

Patty: Aahahah.

Chris: The hell are you laughing at, Jamal? Yeah, I may be twenty-seven years old with the knees and back of a seventy-seven year old man, but yo momma damn near was in the same class as Morgan freeman and is out here giving three for ten dollar hand jobs behind the 7/11 every Thursday and two for five dollars on Sundays.

Jamal: You ain't right.

Patty: And that's why people do not crack jokes with the Army men.

Lisa: Well damn that hurt man, hahahaha.

LJ: Shit man, damn, I surrender.

Tracey: Um… does she do women too or just men, because I mean it's been a while an those prices got damn, hahahaha.

Jamal: *Gives Tracey an evil stare*

Ahaha I quit.

Chris: Hahahahaha, what I thought, don't get butt hurt boys it's all jokes. Hahaha, just next time try harder I am the king for a reason.

Chapter 3
The Car Ride

Chris: Alright, now that everyone is here finally… ***glaces at LJ*** … and the jokes are out of the way.

LJ: Love you, too, boo boo Mcstink stink.

Lisa: Ya can be gay somewhere else please, and thank you.

LJ: Don't hate because you don't have a love like ours.

Lisa: One, my wife and I love each other far better than your two bromance love. Two, my wife looks better than ya. Three, go drink some dirty bath water.

Jamal: I got some dirty bathwater you can drink…

Silence takes over the room and everyone looks at Jamal

LJ: Aye yoo.

Shocked face

Jamal: Now shut up, I'm ready to drive to the campsite, drink, and relax.

Chris: Alrighty then, so we have two trucks outside already loaded with all our stuff. LJ, don't worry, your bags got loaded already.

LJ: Thanks bro, whoever made this food is good as hell!

Patty: Happy you like it.

Chris: Now who's riding with who is the big question…

Jamal: Whoever rides with me all I ask is don't spill food or drink, if you do, please clean it up. We're not kids here people.

Chris: I agree with Jamal, if you spill it, clean it.

Everyone agrees

Lisa: I'm going to ride with Jamal.

Tracey: I too will ride with Jamal

LJ: Just like old times, am I right?

Jamal: Seem like it since that last time you rode in my truck you threw up.

Chris: Yeah, see LJ, you better not throw up in my truck or else I'll make you eat it!

LJ: Sir, now let me explain why I threw up…

All eyes on LJ

LJ: And before anyone of ya thought it had something to do with alcohol, it wasn't that. Jamal and I were playing basketball and I was cooking him.

Jamal: Now you know that is a lie.

LJ: Alright, alright, he was cooking me, but I was making a comeback.

Lisa: Okay?!?! So why did you throw up in Jamal truck?

LJ: Well Ms. Rude, I threw up because…

Jamal interrupts LJ

Jamal: A long story short, jackass over there drank water too fast and it came back to get him and threw up in the front seat.

Chris: LJ, yo ass sitting in the back, and Patty you can ride shotgun.

 LJ: Fine by me, that just means I get to lay in the back and sleep… ***starts to daydream*** …and I get to see Patty. God, I missed her so much and I can't stop thinking about that night…

Chris: *Breaks up LJ's daydreaming by calling his name three times* LJ, LJ, LJ!

LJ: Jackass say what?

Chris: Huh now, come on man, everyone is in the cars waiting and I have to lock up so we can head on out.

LJ: Okay.

heads out of the house and heads to truck

Chris: This mofo better not… ***hears truck door slam*** …slam my door… I should whoop his ass or better yet I have a better idea.

Locks door and walks to truck and climbs inside

Aye, LJ.

LJ: Aye, Chris.

Chris: You forgot your herpes medicine in the room.

tosses pill bottle at LJ

Patty: Someone's been busy I see, hahaha.

LJ: What?!?! NO, I don't have herpes!

Catches bottle

You ass, this is Tylenol.

Patty: *Dying of Laughter*

That was too funny, Chris, LJ better take the medicine before you flair up.

Patty begins to laugh again. Cracking of the walkie talkie stops Chris and Patty's laughter

Lisa: Hey are you guys ready? Tracey is sleeping already and Jamal is done picking his playlist. ***over***

Chris: *wipes his face from the tears*

Yeah, we're ready… ***starts to cough and clears throat*** Yeah we're ready, let's start up and head out.

Jamal: *Grabs walkie*

What the hell are you guys laughing at?

LJ: *Yells* Nothing!

Patty: I wasn't holding the talking button so they didn't hear you… ***chuckles a bit and then hits the button*** Nothing, just laughing at LJ's herpes.

Jamal and Lisa: *Both speak at the same time* His what?!?!

Cars rolling down the road

LJ: I hate both of you, I hope you know that!

Patty: Awww, come on LJ, it was funny.

LJ: Yeah, sure… Anyway how much farther, man?

Chris: Well the GPS says about two hours and fifteen minutes to get to the initial camping area, and then another one to two hour drive in the woods to get to our spot. So in total three hours and forty-five mins to four hours.

Jamal: Aye, man, we got to make a pit stop. Tracey got to pee, Lisa and I had to stretch my legs. An got to make sure herpes boy is okay. ***starts laughing***

LJ: *Takes walkie from Chris*

I'm going to shove my big toe so far up yo ass my toenail will be your new wisdom tooth.

Jamal: *Holds talk button*

Would I catch herpes like that?

 LJ: I hate all of ya.

Everyone starts laughing

Chris: Yeah man, there is a gas station coming up in a couple miles.

Jamal: Okay.

The friends drive another hour to get to the rest stop and start pulling in

Jamal: *Yawning and stretching*

Aw shit, it feels good to stretch these legs of mine

Tracey: *Walking to the bathroom*

I'll be back, I have to tinkle really badly.

LJ: Yeah, I'm going to go pee too.

Chris: Did she just say tinkle?

Jamal: Well I believe she did…

Lisa: What's wrong with that?

Chris: She's a grown woman saying she gotta tinkle, she does better saying she has to pee.

LJ & Tracey walking back to the group

Tracey: Dude, I slept so good that ride up here, why was everyone laughing though?

LJ: What do you mean?

Tracey: I woke up to Jamal and Lisa cracking up laughing so hard Lisa was crying. So what was the joke?

LJ: Chris took a Tylenol bottle from his house and got in the truck and tossed it to me in the back seat saying you forgot your herpes medicine in the house in front of Patty. And then she said it to Jamal and Lisa, so yeah they're joking about me having herpes.

Tracey: *Also had a good poker face*

Well, do you?!

LJ: Hell no!

Tracey: *No longer able to control herself*

HAHAHAHAHAHAHAHA!

Tracey and LJ make it back to the group of friends while Tracey slows her laughing

Patty: What's so funny?

Tracey: LJ told me what Chris did, genius, hahaha.

Chris: Thank you. But anyway, in all seriousness family is everyone good, and ready to head out?

Jamal: Yeah, I'm good

Patty: I'm fine.

LJ: I'm set.

Tracey: I'm ready to eat, but yeah, I'm ready to get on the road again.

Lisa: Yeah, I'm ready.

As the group of friends head back to the trucks the Park Ranger pulls in and stops them

Park Ranger 1: Hey folks quick second.

The group stops

Chris: Anything we can help you with, Ranger?

Park Ranger 1: Yes, if you don't mind answering a few questions…

Chris: Sure, no problem.

Park Ranger 1: Okay, great, I am Park Ranger Elliott and this is my partner, Stacey.

Everyone greets the Rangers

Ranger Elliott: Hello everyone, so I see you guys are camping up here, do you mind me asking how long?

Chris: About three, maybe four days, five the max.

Ranger Stacey: Do you guys have any firearms?

Chris: Yes, I have my AR-15 and, Jamal, do you have your 12-gauge?

Jamal: Yes, I do, is there an issue with us having these, Rangers?

Ranger Stacey: No, not at all, we ask because we've been hearing a lot of shots at night and trying to track the shooters down but when we find the area of the shooting we only come across shell casings, it is always footprints running in all directions.

Ranger Elliott: Well we know it wasn't you folks but if you see anything please call us.

Chris: We will thank you Rangers.

Park Rangers headi toward pick-up truck

Lisa: That was weird.

Tracey: Yeah, it was, but who would come to the woods just to shoot and then leave?

LJ: It is weird, but I am heading back to the truck and taking a nap.

Jamal: Yeah, I'm ready to hit the road too.

Chris: Same.

Everyone gets into trucks and heads out

Chris: Aye, LJ.

LJ: Yoooo.

Chris: Tell Patty and I a poem, I know you still write.

Patty: Oh yeah, I remember when he won the poetry slam and the open mic two years in a row.

LJ: But I'm tired.

Chris: Just one, maybe two, yeah two, but one for now.

Patty: Please!

LJ: Ugh, fine give me a second and let me think… this is from another friend of mine but…

"Dark days have the brightest morning

Pain is not permanent but my love for you is

I can't promise that I'll be perfect for you but…

My thoughts of you are

I can see you in a wedding dress walking down the aisle to me

Because I'm only for you

Just like you're the last person in the supermarket this register is just for you

My last name is only for you until we have little ones and I have to share them with you

I hope they look like you because when you're at work

An I get the kids to myself and it's like looking at you

When you're not around

I want to grow old and gray with you

Hug, fight, kiss on you

Pick you up when you're down

And then lay you down

LJ didn't realize Chris kept glancing in the rear-view mirror and saw him staring at Patty and out the corner of his eye saw Patty blushing

LJ: Yeah, happy now? And now I'm going to sleep to wake me up when we're there.

Chris: *Didn't mention what he saw to the two just ignored it*

Yeah, bro, I will.

CHAPTER 4
THE CAMPSITE

Chris: *holds talk button*

Aye guys, we're finally here!

Jamal: *holds talk button*

About time, man! So how are we going to do this when it comes to parking the trucks?

Lisa: Why don't we park them both facing the exit, the way we came in so it's easier for us to get out when it's time to head home?

Chris: That doesn't sound like a bad idea, to be honest. Let's make it happen.

As the guys, Chris and Jamal, are staging the trucks, Lisa, Patty, and LJ are setting tents and Tracey is collecting firewood before the sun goes all the way down when…

Tracey: *Screams*

Ahhhhhhhhhhhhhh!

Everyone runs to the sound of their friend screaming for her life

Jamal: TRACEY!!!

Chris: WHERE are you?!?!?

Tracey: Over here!

As the rest of the friends bust through the bushes where Tracey is, they found out why she was screaming bloody murder…

Lisa: Oh my God, Tracey, are you okay?

Tracey: Yeah, I'm fine, I almost stepped in it.

Jamal: Damn, what in the world happened here?!?!

LJ: Not sure, but I do not want to find out what or who did it and I for damn sure don't want to be around if they or it comes back!

Patty: Hey Tracey, come, let's head back to camp I'll pick up the rest of the fire wood you found already.

And as soon as Patty said that they didn't notice what Tracey fire wood landed on and covered up.

Noticed it first and did everything he could to stop Patty from touching it.

Chris: Patty, listen to me, I'll get to wood don't worry about it okay, do not touch it.

Patty: I got it, don't worry. I'm fine.

Patty goes to pick up the bundle of sticks and leaves. She feels and now understands why Chris told her not to touch it… Patty screams and everyone panics.

Jamal: Oh shit, Patty, drop it!

Frozen in shock, she just stands there holding a deer head in her arms dripping of blood and muscle. Thinking fast, LJ dashes over to her and knocks it out her arms and holds her, getting blood on his shirt.

LJ: Hey, hey, hey, it's okay. I got you, everything is alright.

Chris: Alright, I'll get fresh leaves, sticks, and wood for the fire, and you guys head back to camp.

Everyone heads back to camp, but Jamal stays behind a bit to talk to Chris.

Jamal: Aye, man.

Chris: Yeah?

Jamal: Great way to start our friends' reunion camping trip, am I right?

Chris: Yeah, hahaha, hopefully the girls will be okay.

Jamal: Yeah, I hope so too, but hey, check this out. I can't shake the feeling we're being watched.

Chris: Yeah, I had that feeling as well.

Jamal: Okay, as long as I'm not the only one feeling like that. What should we do?

Chris: Keep it on low but keep your eyes open.

Jamal: Bet!

Both men start walking back to camp.

LJ: Tracey, you okay?

Tracey: Yeah, I'll be fine. Patty? Hun, you okay?

Patty: *still a bit shaken*

Hmm… yeah I I I... ***clears throat*** I'll be okay.

LJ: You sure?

Patty: Yeah, I'm sure. Did anyone bring anything to "drink" or to smoke? That'll help me take my mind off of things.

LJ: Yeah, I do, let me go change my shirt and go in my bag in the tent and get it.

Gets up and heads to the boys' tent.

Chris and Jamal return with leaves, sticks, and wood and start to make a fire.

Jamal: Tracey and Patty, how are you girls doing?

Tracey: I'm doing better now.

Patty: I'm doing okay, about to head to the girls tent and wipe my arms off and change my shirt. ***Gets up and heads to girls' tent***

Lisa: So are you guys going to smoke a little and sip some drink with us or too scared like you guys were in college? Well, Jamal, I know you might drink, but Chris never really drank with us.

Chris: Well now that I'm done with the military and nothing lined up that'll drug test me, sure, I'll smoke a little something something.

Jamal: Nice, this will be interesting, hahaha.

LJ: *Sees Patty heading to the tent and follows her*

Hey Patty… Patty?

Patty: Yeah, who's there?

LJ: It's me, LJ, just coming to check on you.

Patty: Oh, come in, I'm wiping the blood off my arms.

As LJ walks in he's hit with Patty being shirtless and looks away and starts to blush.

Patty: It's okay to look, not like you never seen me naked before, LJ. But can I ask you something?

LJ: *looks at Patty and starts to remember the things they did in their dorm rooms*

Yeah, Patty, you're right. I've seen you naked and really missed the things we've done with one another. If only everyone wasn't around… ***fantasizing about touching Patty*** But what's your question?

Patty: That poem you said in the car, was that about me?

LJ: Yeah, it was, how'd you know?

Patty: Because one night while you were sleeping I saw your poetry book open and I read it. I've always loved you… I mean your poems. I've always loved your poems.

LJ: Patty, I've always loved you since high school and college and seeing you now makes me want you even more than ever!

LJ & Patty don't realize their walking and getting closer to one another

LJ places his hands on Patty's Coke bottle waist and Patty places her soft hands on his face lightly pulling him in to kiss when…

Lisa: *Walks into the tent*

Oh, um, am I interrupting something here?

LJ: *Drops his hands from Patty's waist*

Oh ***clears his throat*** No, Lisa, you're not I was ugh… just leaving

LJ proceeds to walk out the women's tent and looks back at Patty and Lisa and lets the flap go.

Lisa: So what was that?

Patty: Huh?!?! What was what?

Lisa: I must have stupid written on my forehead or something you know what I am talking about.

Patty: *sighs*

Okay, okay, okay, promise not to tell the others!

Lisa: I promise!

Patty: LJ and I have a thing going on, and it's been going on for a while now…

Lisa: Oh my gosh, oh my gosh, oh my gosh! Why didn't you tell anyone?

Patty: Well because if things ended badly we didn't want the group to break up.

Lisa: That makes sense, but wait for me please, I want to put some warmer clothes on.

Patty: Okay.

Chapter 5
Red Eyes

LJ: Okay, now that we have everyone here at the fire, I got the weed rolled up and ready, and cups for that drank you know what I'm saying.

Everyone is excited and ready to have a good time and laughs and cheers for seeing the alcohol and weed.

LJ: Alright, in honor of the great Chris for serving this "Great Country of Ours" and coming back to us alive I say he gets the first shot and pull of the joint. What do you guys think, huh?

Everyone says yeah to what LJ proposed.

Chris: Umm, okay, haha, shot first.

LJ pours Chris a shot, Chris throws it back feeling the burn going down to his stomach reminding him how just a couple days ago he was drinking alone and remembering the gun firing going pass his head and trying to save a good friend he met while serving in the military.

LJ: Alright, now time for the blunt. Now just go easy we don't want you to fall or anything.

Chris: *Takes the blunt and tries smoking it*

cough cough cough

Holy shit, man

cough cough cough

Jamal: Good shit, Chris, hahaha.

Tracey: Get him some water, hahaha.

Lisa: Welcome to the club, Chris, haha.

Patty: He took a hit of the weed way too hard, but aye at least he didn't chicken out and kept making excuses on why he can't smoke ***cough cough*** Jamal.

Tracey: Oh damn, I do remember that, haha, my favorite lie he said was, hahah,he "can't smoke because his dog would get contact high and then set the fire alarm off."

LJ: Mofo… what? Hahaha.

Jamal: Aye man, don't judge me. Let's not forget how LJ was when he was drunk for the first time with us.

LJ: Feeling embarrassed, yeah, yeah, let us not talk about.

Jamal: Oh na, let us talk about it, with your simple ass mixing light and dark after us telling you it is bad but what you tell us?

Tracey: Hahaha, he said, and I quote, "momma ain't raise no bitch gimme them shits"

Chris: Hahaha, I remember that because we had to stop him from fighting a tree because he thought it was a person.

Lisa: But here's my question, LJ, Hahaha.

LJ: Yes?

showing embarrassment of the memory the group is talking about

Lisa: How do you fight a tree and lose?

Everyone starts dying laughing

LJ: *Mocking their laughter*

Hahahaha, shut the hell up.

Patty: Aww, don't be so butt hurt, it's in our memories forever. I wish I got the trees trainer though.

More laughter comes about

LJ: I hate you guys, but love ya.

Chris: We love you, too.

More drinking but less smoking continues.

Jamal: Aye, I'm going to take a tinkle, hahaha, right Tracey?

Tracey: Yeah, that right tinkle, but I suggest you go pee before I tell everyone what I caught you doing on Snapchat before you deleted the video!

Jamal: Shut up!

Walks into woods beyond the groups' sight

She better not tell them nothing if she does I have nothing back to counter her… Damn, ***unzips pants and starts peeing*** This is nice, this is great ***shakes and zips pants up.***

Off in the distance Jamal can faintly hear growling and see what he thinks are red eyes slowly getting closer to him.

Jamal: What the actual fuck is that...

Backing up away from the spot where he peed

 Bruh I got to get out of here

As this thing got closer Jamal hears a stick break and then turns and hails ass back towards the group. When he makes it he is drenched in sweat trying to catch his breath.

Chris: Wow, man, wow, take it easy, focus on breathing!

Lisa: Everyone, back up and give him some room so he can breathe. Patty, can you get him some water?

Patty: Yeah, sure

Grabs water bottle and hands it over to Jamal who's starting to catch his breath

Jamal starts to catch his breath and calms down

Chris: What did you see?

Jamal: I saw red eyes and heard growling around me, and I tried to stay calm until I heard a branch break in front of me and I took off!

LJ: I mean of course you're going to see red eyes. We are in the deep woods camping.

Jamal: *drinks more water*

Yeah, I know, but these eyes were chilling to the bone, I felt stuck like I couldn't look away at all.

LJ: Yeah, no more weed for you.

Jamal: *Noticingly getting angry*

Bro, what the fuck?!?! I know what I saw!

LJ: I don't know who the hell you think you're talking to, but it isn't me!

Jamal: Bitch, I am talking to you!

Jamal starts walking up on LJ

LJ: *Puts his hands up*

Bet, let's do this then... ***walks close to Jamal***

Patty: Guys, chill out, we're not doing this right now! LJ, shut up! Jamal, you too!

Chris: Ya need to chill out, man!

Tracey: Chill the hell out and get away from each other!

As the two grown men are about to come to blows they hear a gunshot off in the distance

Lisa: What was that...

Chris: Sounded like...

More shots going off in the distance

Tracey: They sound far away but we can hear them. Why is that?!?! Is there a shooting range here?!

Chris: When there is no surrounding you can hear them from a mile or two away and depending on the caliber of gun maybe more.

Lisa: Okay, well what was that because I'd hate to get hit with a stray bullet...

Chris: I don't know but look a lot has happened tonight let us all get some sleep and go for a hike in the morning, okay?

Tracey: Yeah, I agree.

Lisa: Okay.

Patty: Sure, LJ and Jamal shake hands and do not do anything stupid to ruin this trip!

Tracey: Yeah, LJ apologize to Jamal for not acknowledging what just happened and Jamal apologize to LJ because you were about to fight someone that has a hard time walking and chewing gum...

Jamal: *chuckles* You right, LJ, my bad bro, just what I saw really made the hairs on my neck stand up and the only thing in my mind was to get away...

LJ: It's cool, man, I shouldn't have tried to make fun of you seeing that you were literally scared out of your mind. Oh and Tracey...

Tracey: Yes?

LJ: There's a spider on your foot…

Tracey: *Screams* Look down… No, there's not!

LJ ran into the tent laughing

Chris: Alright guys, let's get some sleep, hahaha, goodnight guys.

Lisa: Night.

Jamal: Goodnight.

Tracey: I'm going to kill him, goodnight.

Patty: Haha, night.

Chapter 6
The Hike

LJ: *Starts singing* It's seven o'clock on the dot

I'm in this tent with Jamal and Chris

Bow bow boow

I don't wanna go on this hike but they're making meeeee

I rather be snuggled up baby

And smoking my weed oooo yeah... I had plans oof waking and baking

But now "mmm gettin up and dressed to go walking with my friennnnds

They are called L...U... I... S big pot head

Over trying to get high in bed but that ain't happening

As LJ was about to start singing Jamal interrupts him

Jamal: LJ...

LJ: Yeah, snuggle bear?

Jamal: Shut the fuck up.

Chris: But I like that song.

Patty: We do too.

Jamal: Do not feed into his antics please…

LJ: But it's a number one hit though.

Jamal: Yeah, the number one that will get you hit in the morning…

Chris: Is everyone up and ready,? We all know Jamal is not a morning person.

Patty: Yeah, I guess that never changed, hahaha, but yes us ladies are ready, sergeant.

Chris: Good because now as usual we're waiting on LJ. Man, how he takes longer than the women I'll never know.

Tracey: Okay, Mr. Misogynist …

Chris: It's not like that but …

Tracey: But what?!

Jamal: Women do take a long time when it comes to getting ready, picking places to eat, and then get mad at their partner if they have to wait five minutes for them. Tell me I'm wrong.

Patty: You're wrong.

LJ: How is he?!?

Patty: I mean he is, but he isn't wrong because depending on the situation everyone takes a long time and he said tell me I am wrong so I did. ***smiles***

LJ: Hahaha, very funny.

Chris: Now, now, now ladies, you're all pretty and all the boys want you, can we go now?

Everyone: Yeah, let's go.

Everyone heads north

Thirty minutes into hike

Tracey: How much longer, ughhhhhh.

Patty: Girl, it has only been, what, thirty minutes? We should be almost there, whatever there is. Right, Chris?

Chris: *singing Army cadences in his head*

Your mother was home when you left you're right, your father was home when you left you're right, your brother was home when you left you're right, your sister was home when you left you're right, your son was home when you left you're right, your daughter was home when you left you're right, your mother your father your son your daughter was home the day that you left you're right and that's the reason you left you're right, I left my ho…

Patty: *Yells* CHRIS!!!!

Everyone looks to see why Patty is yelling

Chris: *knocked out his trace*

Hmmmm, yeah, what's up?

Patty: How much longer, man? My legs are killing me.

Chris: *checks watch*

It's only been thirty minutes, hahaha. Your legs need a break already?

LJ: Damn, didn't realize we've been walking that long.

Chris: Yeah man, oh man, do you see this view?!

Tracey: Yeah, this is beautiful. Oh my God.

Jamal: Man, oh man, not going to lie, I didn't want to go on this hike, but Chris, got to give it to you this was a good idea.

Chris: Thank you, do you want to keep heading up the mountain?

Lisa: I think I can speak for everyone when I say this… No, no we do not want to keep going up the mountain, haha.

Patty: Maybe if I wasn't hungry and had better shoes to hike in maybe I'd be down to keep going, but I'd rather head back to camp and relax and cook something, but let me head to a bush and relieve myself right quick.

Chris: Okay, we'll be here waiting for you to get back.

Patty: Do any of the girls care to come with me?

LJ: What is the matter, going to pee in the woods by yourself? Hahaha, thought you were tough and not scared of anything? Guess not.

Jamal: I'd leave her alone if I was you.

Tracey: Yeah, remember what happened when she and Jamal wrestled hahaha.

LJ: Oh yeah, it's weird how fast she is, how fast he tapped…

Jamal: Yeah, let's not bring that up.

Patty: Okay, since no one answered and you guys are going down memory lane I am going to the bathroom.

Patty walks away to use the bathroom

Patty: This fool trying to walk us to death I swear. Okay this is a good spot to pee.

Patty begins to relieve herself

This is a lot better.

Wrestling can be heard in the bushes near Patty along with low growling

Patty: That fake ass growl isn't scaring anyone …

Growling gets louder

Patty: *heart is starting to race her gut is telling her she is in real danger*

Okay, I'm out of here...

Patty begins to run away

The bushes behind her explode as something was chasing her

At this moment Patty is saying to herself Don't look back, don't look back.

Four paws charging at her closing the distance at a very fast

Patty: *Screams*

HELP ME!!!!

Patty busts through the branches where everyone was waiting for her to return

Oh my God, oh my God, GUYS!

Lisa: Patty, what is wrong?

LJ: What happened?!

Tracey: Calm down, you're safe now.

Jamal: Patty, what are you running from?!

Chris: *Pulls out pistol and chambers a round* Everyone get down now!

Everyone gets low

And a couple seconds later a dog with a park ranger vest around him barking and footsteps and yelling not too far from the dog.

Everyone looks at Patty

Patty: What... look don't say nothing.

LJ: Scared of dogs are we now? Hahahaha.

Chris: LJ, leave her alone.

Chris hands Patty some water

Drink this and catch your breath. You're safe from the evil doggy, ha-haha. No, but seriously, what did you think was chasing you?

Jamal: Yeah, because you were screaming as if something was going to kill you or something. You didn't look to see what was chasing you?

Patty: Look my gut was telling me it was something not right and I refuse to be like those dumbasses in the movies going to investigate what was the noise only to end up dead.

Lisa walks over to the dog

Lisa: Aww he's so cute, but where are the park rangers?

Tracey: Yeah… Why would he be out here by himself?

Chris: I do not want to be that guy, but maybe we should head in the direction Patty and the dog came from. Maybe the rangers are in that area looking for him.

LJ: Bruh, it is weird that he's out here all alone, but you know what they say, all dogs find their way home. So maybe we should go to the campsite and eat and hang out there. Besides, we haven't eaten yet so I vote to head back to camp.

Jamal: Yeah, man, for once I agree with LJ on this one, we don't know if this dog was trained or told to do something.

Chris: You both make strong points, but something just doesn't feel right.

And at that moment everyone hears

A voice: *Yells*

LUUUUUCKY … LUUUUUCKY!

Lisa: Is that the dog's name?

Chris: *looks at dogs vest*

Yes, it is.

A Voice: LUUUUUCKY... LUUUUCKY!

Jamal: He's over here!

Patty: Jamal!!!

Jamal: What?

Patty: We do not know who that person is calling for this dog and what they have with them.

Jamal: You're right, but it sounds like the park rangers from yesterday though.

Lisa: He's right.

LJ: Well we'll find out soon because they're coming this way now.

And through the bushes out comes Park Ranger Stacey

CHAPTER 7
THE SECRET

Park Ranger Stacey: *Walks through the bushes*

Hello, everyone, I see you found Lucky.

LJ: Yeah, well technically Lucky found Patty, scared her half to death and chased her here, hahaha.

Patty: Hey, LJ, I'm three seconds from whooping your ass!

Park Ranger Stacey: I do apologize for that, we were on a patrol after hearing gunshots last night and decided to come out and comb the areas.

Chris: If you don't mind me asking, why did you guys choose to come in the morning and not when you first heard it?

Park Ranger Stacey: It's easier to get lost at night in these woods versus during the day and the nighttime predators, even though it's not a lot of them, rather not give them the advantage of getting Lucky or myself or Park Ranger Elliott. Speaking of which, have you guys seen him or heard him by chance? He hasn't called on the radio for about two hours now and we're supposed to check in every hour and then Lucky ran off. So I guess you can say it's been a crazy morning.

Jamal: Sadly, no we haven't seen him.

Tracey: But we did hear the shots last night too. Should we be worried, is there illegal hunting going on here?

Park Ranger Stacey: Not sure of illegal hunting but definitely strange.

Chris: Why is that?

Park Ranger Stacey: So I am not supposed to share this with you guys because I do not want to scare you guys, but we did find a deer carcass ripped to shreds. Half-eaten body parts everywhere, with wolf prints everywhere.

Lisa: But that doesn't explain the gunshots.

Park Ranger Stacey: Well it is illegal to hunt deer and last year we caught over twenty people illegally hunting and we think that they're maybe people up here hunting illegally and as they go and collect the deer that wolves smell the blood and try to take the easy kill.

Chris: Well that does kind of make sense. Why hunt for the food when you can either bully someone for their kill or even get two kills and a plus one so you can eat till you're full?

LJ: As amazing as this mystery is and truly am intrigued, the urge to is very strong.

Tracey: Yeah, I now agree with LJ, plus my feet hurt and I'd like to relax.

Park Ranger Stacey: Okay, sorry to take up your guys time and thank you for keeping Lucky with you. Please be safe and keep your eyes open and if you hear and or see something please call us ASAP!

Chris: Can do, what is the number?

Park Ranger Stacey: It is 857-345-3511.

Radio crackles

Park Ranger Elliott: Stacey… Stacey, where are you?!

Radio crackles

Before Stacey could say anything

Radio crackles again

Get back to the station now!

Park Ranger Stacey: On the way! See you folks later!

Everyone says goodbye and the friends head back to camp as the ranger and Lucky head back to their headquarters.

Patty: Finally, after all that walking we're finally back to camp. Time to take these boots off and relax.

LJ: I second that one.

Chris: I'm going to head to the truck and get the mini grill out and start cooking the hot dogs and burgers.

Jamal: Need any help?

Chris: Yeah, I can use some to make things go faster.

Lisa: Are you sure that it's a good idea we cook meat while these wolves are taking people?

LJ: I'm pretty sure Chris has enough ammo to put them down if need be and we all need to eat. We've been up since seven A.M. and it's almost three P.M. We have to eat. We'll just have to make sure we kill the smell and smoke when we are done.

Jamal: You know it is kind of scary sometimes when LJ uses his brain.

Tracey: Jamal, you make a valid point.

Chris: Okay, let's hurry up and get cooking and drinking.

Patty: Let's do it!

As Chris is cooking and everyone is laughing and enjoying the food, time slips from their minds which later they will realize it was a grave mistake.

Chris: Damn, the sun is almost down. Is everyone done eating?

LJ: Yeah.

Tracey: Yes.

Patty: Yeah.

Jamal: Yup.

Lisa: Yeah.

Chris: Okay.

 Chris grabs the water, dumps it on the grill, and puts dirt over the smoke

LJ: Man, Chris, you can cook, bro, forreal!

Chris: Thanks, man.

Jamal: Where did you learn how to cook and make the flavor pop like that?

Chris: When you're sitting around all day waiting for orders you tend to watch a lot of pointless videos and a lot of those videos tend to be cooking videos.

Jamal: I'll be back. I am going to run to the tent and add some layers, not sure why I got cold all of sudden.

Tracey: So what was it like being in the Army for so long?

Chris: To be honest with you, I loved it and hated it at the same time.

Lisa: What do you mean?

Chris: Well I have stories for days, but I'll tell you this, you will meet some amazing people and build a bond like no other and others you want to beat the shit out of but can't because they'll cry and bitch.

And as Chris goes into detail about other things you'll experience in the military, Patty walks away towards the tents and Jamal notices this but says nothing.

Jamal: Man, it got cold, it was strange how park ranger Elliott called back Stacey though I hope everything is okay… I've known Patty for years and I've never seen her that scared, shit out of everyone. I have her backing down a bear before she turns and tries to get away.

As Jamal gets closer he can hear whispers and lips smacking as if they're coming together.

Jamal: Am I hearing things or is that kissing noises. *** Looks around*** Wait, didn't LJ and Patty have been gone for a while now? They couldn't be…

Jamal walks around the car slowly and he can not believe what he is seeing.

Jamal: ***Clears throat***

Don't mind me just getting my jacket.

Both Patty & LJ panic

Patty: Oh my God, oh my God, um I'm going to the others, excuse Jamal…

LJ: ***Looking at Jamal with a scared face***

It wasn't what it looked like…

Jamal: Bro, I've been drinking, its cold, I didn't see shit.

LJ: Seriously?

Jamal: Not going to lie to you, bro, I saw and heard it all, but you know what I am going to say what Ray Charles used to say, man.

LJ: What's that?

Jamal: I didn't see nothing, so I can't say anything.

LJ: Please do not say anything to anyone else, man.

Jamal: I won't, man, but curious how long this has been going on?

LJ: To be honest… well first you can't say nothing to anyone like no one, the rest doesn't know like seriously put it on something so I know you won't tell anyone .

Jamal: *sigh* Fine, I put that on everything I love. I won't say anything.

LJ: Okay… Well the one night I did an open mic night and ya didn't come. Patty did come, and man she had me tongue tied, like star struck. I felt weird seeing her in her dress that she wore, and after I performed her and I went for a walk and was just walking and talking and one thing lead to another we ended up back in my dorm. And her and I agreed to keep it on the downlow because if her and I made it public and broke up because college life will do that to a happy couple sometimes, I eventually broke things off completely because I would rather be in her life forever as a friend than make things awkward as a fail relationship you know?

Jamal: So in a sense, friends with benefits, no strings attached?

LJ: In a sense, yes, and when everyone was attacking me in the room at Chris' house, all those memories and feelings came back, and it's been hard trying not to touch her like a dog trying not to eat food on the floor.

Jamal: Damn, I mean that makes sense, but I'll keep my mouth shut.

Chris walks into the tent

Chris: Keep your mouth shut about what?

LJ: NOTHING… it's nothing.

Chris: Umm, okay.

Jamal: Don't worry, Chris, it really is nothing. We were heading back to the fire and you just caught us off guard.

Chris: Oh, my bad I guess, but yeah everyone went to sleep or at least headed to sleep. The ladies went to their tent and you two was taking forever to come back. Patty also seemed kind of nervous or scared of something. Was everything okay?

Before LJ can answer, Jamal intervened

Jamal: Yeah, I just said she had a big ass bug on her and she froze is all.

She'll be fine. But since no one is out there I'm going to lay down. Goodnight, boys.

LJ: Night, man.

Chris: Night.

Chapter 8

The Fight Begins

1:47 A.M.

Jamal: *crying* I'm sorry, man... I'm sorry.

LJ: *Breathing heavily and slowly laying in Jamal's arms*

Hey man, what are you sorry for... **cough cough**

Patty: *applying pressure to the giant slash across LJ's chest and trying to hold back her tears*

Guys, help me please... LJ, you're going to be okay, just stay awake please stop talking!

Chris being in this type of situation before already knew LJ without real medical attention would not make another ten minutes

Patty, he's gone...

Patty: What do you mean... He's still with us... he's still...

Patty looks up to see LJ's eyes are closed and she doesn't feel a pulse anymore, and that's when it truly sets in and the tears start running down her face as she realizes LJ the love of her life is now gone

This cannot be happening right now, not like this...

Chris: We have to go!

Patty: And what about LJ?

Chris: LJ is gone and to carry his body now we most definitely get us all killed! Listen, LJ was my friend, more than a friend he was my damn brother ***fighting the urge of crying, wipes his face*** but we will come back for his body later but we need to find help and find it sooner than later before it comes back!

hissing noise can be heard

Chris: Do you guys hear that?

Lisa: *crying*

Hear what?

Chris: A hissing noise like something losing air?

Tracey: *sniffling*

Wake up, Chris…

Lisa: Wake up, Chris.

Chris: Huh, why are…?

Jamal: Wake up, Chris. ***going on outside the tent near the cars***

Chris is woken up by the noise

Chris: What the hell is that noise?

silence, the hissing noise continues

What the hell is that noise? Aye Jamal… LJ… Jamal… LJ! You heavy sleeping stupid jackasses, WAKE UP!

Jamal: Who are you calling a jackass?!

Chris: Shush and listen

Hissing noise lowering

Jamal: Who are you calling a stupid jackass?!

LJ: Ladies… ladies, you're both beautiful now please let me return to my beautiful wife in my dreams calling me back to her.

Hissing noise became louder

LJ: What is that hissing noise?

Chris: We don't know.

Jamal: Rattlesnake?

LJ: Excuse me?

Chris: I do not think so. It's too cold for them right now.

Hissing fading away

Jamal: Whatever it was it sounds like it is going away.

Radio cracking

Lisa: Hey guys… please be awake… guys there's growling at our tent. Hello?!?!

Chris: Yeah, we're up and okay, but Lisa you have to say over so I know when you're done talking. Over.

Lisa: Chris, this is not the time for your military talk shit! Something is outside the tent!… OVER.

Chris: Okay, we're getting dressed now! Aye ya heard her!

Jamal: Bro, what are we going to do if it's a bear?!

LJ: Good question!

Chris: Depending on what kind of bear we make ourselves sound and look big and it'll run away.

LJ: And if that doesn't work?!

Jamal: Then we'll feed you to the bear.

Chris: Jamal, this is not a time to make jokes. On the count of three we'll run out, make noise, and think and be big, okay?

LJ & Jamal: Bet!

Chris: One... Two...

LJ: Shit, I'm scared.

Chris: Three!

The men burst out of their tent screaming and waving their arms around like crazy men, and at that moment whatever was at the women's tent ran off into the woods.

Jamal: That thing was huge.

Tracey: *yells from the tent*

That's what she said.

laughter

Chris: You guys can come out now.

Girls come out the tent

Lisa: Did you guys get a chance to see what it was?

LJ: The way it looked from it running away probably a bear, to be honest.

Patty: I don't know, it was acting like a bear.

Tracey: Listen, I can tell you how a car is supposed to sound while it is running but I don't know how bears are supposed and aren't supposed to act. So I am going to use the bathroom really fast. ***Walks away***

LJ: Man, you guys should've heard Jamal in the tent when we heard hissing, haha, man was scared as hell. Was that a rattlesnake? Hahaha.

Slight laughter

Jamal: *Feeling embarrassed*

Bruh, why do you think everything is a damn joke!

LJ: Man, Jamal, calm down whatever was near we scared away, learn to take a joke. You can dish it but can't take it, get your thong out your ass!

Jamal: Watch your mouth!

LJ: Man, what are you going to do?

Jamal: I'm about to…

LJ interrupts Jamal

LJ: About to do nothing but sell wolf tickets your ass can't cash.

Chris: Alright man calm down, it's not that serious.

LJ and Jamal start walking towards one another

Jamal: You know I've been waiting to beat your ass for a long time now!

LJ: You are still talking step up or shut up!

Chris: Will you two cut this shit out!

Tracey: Um, guys …

Lisa: Yeah, Tracey, what's up?

Tracey: Th… there's something looking at us…

Tracey moves slowly to point in the direction in which she is looking as if she was slowly freezing over, finally gets her arm up and points at a beast slowly raising on its back two leg.

Everyone looks frozen as they see what they supposedly chased off was damn near nine feet tall and eyes bloodshot red and teeth whiter than the moon above them all.

Lisa: Oh my God…

LJ: What the hell is that thing…

Chris: Get in the truck. Slowly.

Jamal: What…

Patty: *slowly creeping to the truck* He said, geee…

Before she can finish her sentence the creature roars an eardrum breaking roar and charges at them

Chris: GET IN MY TRUCK!

EVERYONE PILES INTO CHRIS' TRUCK

Chris: Shit… shit… where are the damn keys?!

Jamal: HURRY UP THAT THING is getting…

CRASH, the beast slams into the side of the vehicle with such force almost knocking the big truck on its side.

Everyone is screaming while Chris is trying to find the keys to get everyone to safety.

LJ: Chris, look under the fucking seat!

Chris: *Feels under the seat*

Found them!

Starts the truck and drives off with the beast following behind them!

Jamal: DRIVE FASTER, IT'S CATCHING UP!

Lisa: HERE IT COMES!

CRASHING NOISE

Tracey: IT'S TRYING TO PUSH US OFF THE ROAD!

Chris: Jamal, hold the wheel!

Jamal: WHAT?

Chris: HOLD THE FUCKING WHEEL!

Jamal: *Holds onto the wheel while Chris is adjusting to do something that no one saw coming*

What the fuck are you doing?! Why are we slowing down?!

Chris: JUST HOLD THE WHEEL!

Chris cocking the handgun this time to make sure it fires looks in the side mirror

That's right, come back up here, little bitch!

LJ: HERE IT COMES AGAIN!

Just as the creature was about to make contact with the car Chris shoots four shots hitting the creature three out of the four, making it fall to the ground and slide kicking up dirt.

CHAPTER 9

BROKEN HEARTS

LJ: HOLY SHIT! HOLY SHIT! DID YOU GUYS SEE THAT THING?

Jamal: Chris, man, what a damn shot, you killed!

Tracey: What was that damn thing?!

Lisa: Chris, what was it?

Jamal: Whatever it was, he killed it… right, Chris?

Chris: *With fear in his eyes*

I ugh… I don't know.

Patty: But Chris, when you shot you hit it right?!

Chris: Yeah, I did but…

Jamal: *interrupts Chris* Man, but nothing, you shot it point blank range we saw the body hit the ground and we got away, now let's drive our ass back home. Better the ranger station instead, because I refuse to leave my truck here.

LJ: Not going to lie, I agree with Jamal. Let's get to the park rangers' place and stay there. They should have more guns there, heat, and a phone or something so we can call for help.

Lisa: That sounds like a good idea.

Chris: Yeah, that is a good idea, they should be a couple of miles up the road so we should make it.

thudding noise

LJ: Aye Patty, do you hear that noise?

Thudding noise

Patty: What noise?

Thudding noise

LJ: Just listen.

Thudding noise

Lisa: I kind of hear it too.

Thudding noise increases

LJ: Aye Chris, pull over man, something isn't right with the truck?

Thudding noise

Chris: *Looks at dashboard*

Shit, the tire pressure is low. That must've been the hissing noise we heard at the tents.

Jamal: So what is the plan then?

Chris: *exhales*

Tracey: Please don't say it.

Lisa: Say what?

Chris: We should be good enough distance from whatever that thing was so we should be good. I am going to pull over here. The park ranger spot shouldn't be too far up the road.

Patty: How do you know that?

Chris: We're on the main road, and usually there is a park ranger station not too far from the main road or at least small cabins for emergencies. And if I'm not mistaken there should be a cabin down this road off to the right.

Tracey: Yeah, Chris, you're right. I saw the sign pointing to the right about a ranger cabin this way with an emergency phone inside.

LJ: So we're absolutely doing this… leaving the truck and walking we're not sure how far it is up the road.

Chris: Yeah, that is our best option, unless anyone else has any ideas?

Jamal: Why don't we check the tires to see if they can make it all the way there?

Lisa: Look, we are wasting time. Let's just get out the truck now, speed walk down the road, and hopefully the cabin won't be too far up ahead.

Tracey: Ugh…

Chris: Come, let's hurry up!

Everyone gets out the car and starts speed walking down the road

Patty: Given the situation at hand the night is pretty and the breeze feels good.

Lisa: Yeah, you're not wrong, Patty, I'd have to agree with you.

Jamal: Aye Chris, how much farther up do you think we have to do?

Chris: To be honest, I'm not sure, but I am leaning on not that far because every time we encountered the park rangers it was never too far from our camp or the road. So I guess they're near the road so they can be spotted easier.

Jamal: I mean I guess that makes some type of sense.

The hairs on the back of Chris' neck shot up at attention. Unclear why, he tries to think of what to do next

Chris: Everyone be quiet!

LJ: Are we supposed to hear something?

Chris: I have a bad feeling, and to be honest, yes. It's too quiet, think about it. There's not even crickets making noises.

Lisa: He's right... What should we do?

Chris: I don't know.

LJ: Well we can't stay here.

Walks forward couple feet and a creature comes out the woods and bites down on LJ's shoulder close to his neck and shakes viciously AAAAAAAAHHHHHHHHHHHHHH HELP MEEEEEEEEEEEE! AHAAAAAAAHAHHHHAHAH HELP!

Panic ensues as LJ is being attacked by the creature they thought they got away from

Patty: OH MY GOD!!!!!

Tracey: CHRIS, SHOOT IT!!!!

Chris: I don't have a clean shot!

LJ: AHAHAAAAAAAAAAAAAHHHHHHHHHHHAAA-AHHHHHHH HELP ME PLEASE!

Jamal: WHAT THE FUCK! WHAT THE FUCK! CHRIS, SHOOT IT!

Chris: FUCK!

Starts shooting at the creature attacking LJ

The creature lets go of LJ and tries to get away but...

Click click click goes the gun

Tracey: Is it dead...

Chris: I don't know, looking like it isn't breathing...

LJ: *coughing coughing*

blood rushing from the wound

Baby…

Everyone is confused to who LJ is calling "baby"

Patty: *Crying*

Luis… Luis… Baby…

runs to LJ, grabs his hand, notices that he is bleeding very badly

Patty: *YELLS*

SOMEONE HELP, TRY TO STOP THE BLEEDING!

LJ: *coughing up blood closing his eyes, looks at Patty and smiles*

It's okay, Patty, just know I love you.

Patty: LJ… LJ… no, no, no… please wake up! Please wake up!

Chris: I'm sorry, Patty, he's… he's gone…

Patty: *Yells*

THIS IS ALL YOUR FAULT, CHRIS! FUCK! Why didn't you fucking shoot that damn thing when we told you to!

Chris: I…I… *he stutters* I didn't want to hit him in the crossfire, Patty.

Patty: Bullshit! *crying*

Chris opens his arms and walks towards Patty, hugging her tightly as she cries in his arms after watching her secret boyfriend die.

Jamal: Listen, I know we just lost someone, but we have to go .

Patty: *lifts her head from Chris' chest*

You shut your ass up talking about him… We are not leaving him here!

Lisa: Patty, we have no choice here. We can't take his body, but we can send help to get him back.

Patty: I said NO! I can't leave him here! You all go, I'll stay!

Chris: Patty, listen, I lost one brother I refuse to lose a sister as well. Please let's all go find a phone and safety and we'll get LJ back home and send him home properly, okay?

Patty: *looks into Chris's eyes and realizes that she has to leave the body there, that she isn't the only one that lost someone tonight.*

Fine, but we're not leaving this park without LJ!

Tracey: We won't leave him, come and walk with me, okay?

Patty: Okay, just one second.

Tracey: Okay.

Patty: * Walks to LJ's body and holds his hand*

Hey, baby ***sniffles*** we have to leave you here for now, okay? Just know we'll be back for you and bring you home, okay baby? I love you and will not leave this place until you come home with me. I love you.

Everyone says their goodbyes and starts walking east in the direction they were headed before the attack.

CHAPTER 10

TRUE FEAR SHOWS TRUE COLORS

Tracey: Hey Patty…

Patty: Yeah Tracey…

Tracey: I know with what just happened being fresh and all and hopefully over, I'm curious.

Patty: Of?

Tracey: You and LJ, like how did you two become a thing, you know?

Patty: *chuckles* Oh yeah, well it is kind of funny and like a stupid romantical kind of way.

Tracey: I'm listening…

Patty: Okay, so one night me and my ex-boyfriend Steven were arguing about a bunch of stuff that to me was stupid but of course he wanted to argue about it.

Tracey: I mean if it was bothering him maybe it wasn't stupid.

Patty: I mean I get that but one of things he was going back and forth with me was you guys, especially the guys. His thought process was that a man and woman cannot be friends without sexual tension.

Tracey: Okay, yeah, that is stupid.

Patty: He especially didn't like LJ, like on the verge of wanting to fight, but Steven wasn't about that life.

Tracey: Fight LJ? For what?

Patty: Honestly, I think he felt threatened by LJ for some odd reason.

Tracey: But LJ wouldn't hurt anyone. Yeah, he'd push your buttons but never actually hurt someone.

Patty: That's what I would tell him all the time. Steven was like, why is he always asking you to go get beers?

Tracey: LJ always asks us to get beers though, either he had a long day, a friend had a long day, or he just wanted to drink a beer and have some laughs. It was a secret talent of his.

Patty: Yeah, and that night we were arguing after we got done. LJ texts my phone and asks if I wanted to get a beer, and Steven says, "you go out that door we're done." I said okay, grab my bag, said I'll be back for the rest of my stuff and left.

Tracey: Okay, Ms. Savage, I see you.

Patty: Nah not savage but just don't try to control me and tell me what to do, ya know?

Tracey: Yeah, I can understand that.

Patty: It didn't help that my ex saw a drunk text from LJ he wasn't supposed to see.

Tracey: What? What did it say?

Patty: It said…

Lisa interrupts as Patty as she was about to tell her what LJ texted her

Lisa: Hey, what are you guys talking about?

Tracey: Oh, Patty was telling me about how LJ and her became a thing.

Lisa: Damn, I missed that conversation. ***sucks teeth*** At least ya conversation is a lot better than Jamal's and Chris' convo.

Tracey: What do you mean?

Lisa: Jamal is freaking out after what happened to LJ, that he isn't going out like that and that he isn't going to die in the forest. And those things will not get him and so on just losing it.

Patty: ***Tears up with anger in her eyes***

Fuck Jamal…

Steps on a branch, gun fire erupts from the bushes nearly missing Patty's head, but she drops down to the ground barely just in time. Everyone hits the ground, everyone is screaming and cursing trying to get whoever is shooting to stop.

Chris: WHO EVER IS FUCKING SHOOTING, STOOOOOOOOP!

crawling towards the girls

KEEP YOUR HEADS DOWN!

***Right before Chris raised his firearm to return fire the firing stopped.**

The Voice: Are you man or beast?

Jamal: Who the hell are you?

Tracey: ***whispers***

Jamal, shut the fuck up! He has the upper hand! Don't piss him off and he will kill us!

The Voice: Jamal?!?!

Jamal: Who the fuck are you and how do you know me?!

Park Ranger Elliott: It is me, Ranger Elliott.

Comes around the corner onto the road

Jamal: *Jumps up ready to charge the Park Ranger*

You almost fucking shot us! What the hell is your problem!?

Lisa: Jamal, relax, he didn't know what it was. I'd do the same thing in this situation.

Jamal: Lisa, no one asked you!

Chris: Can we get up?

Park Ranger Elliott: Yes, yes of course. Here let me help you guys.

goes over to help the friends up

Is anyone hurt? Listen, I am so sorry, but those things… Those wolves have been trying to come after.

Chris: We get it, no hard feelings, but we need to get moving. Where did you come from? Is there a cabin nearby we all can hide in to come up with a plan or call for help?

Park Ranger Elliott: Yes, not too far from here. Wait, weren't there six of you guys?

Tracey: He was, um, attacked and killed by a wolf…

Park Ranger Elliott: I am so sorry for your loss. We're kind of in the same boat.

Lisa: Yeah, but what do you mean the same boat?

Park Ranger Elliott: Ranger Stacey was seriously injured when they attacked us on our patrol and Lucky fought hard to try and save us but sadly… they killed her. So now Ranger Stacey is at the cabin trying to heal and pull guard. But we need to leave before…

Howling begins

Jamal: What fucking way do we go?!

Park Ranger Elliott: This way… follow me**!**

starts running towards the cabin

IF I GET TOO FAR THERE IS A TREE WITH A LONG HANGING BRANCH, MAKE A RIGHT AND THE CABIN WILL BE ONE HUNDRED FEET IN FRONT OF YOU!

Chris: COME ON, LET'S GO!

Lisa: HOW MUCH FARTHER TILL THE TREE?

Howling can be heard chasing after everyone

Tracey: FUCK, THEY'RE COMING!

Park Ranger Elliott: THE TREE IS COMING UP… TURN RIGHT HERE!

Lisa: THAT THING IS LOW!

Chris: THAT BRACH IS LOW BE CAREFUL!

Tracey: WAIT FOR ME, PLEASE DO NOT LEAVE ME TO DIE.

Jamal: *Looks back*

RUN FASTER!

Looks back and then forward… CRACK! Falls on his back!*

Ugh shit, my chest…

Tracey: Oh my God, Jamal, are you okay?

Jamal: No, you jackass.

Howling gets more intense

Tracey: I'm going to let that slide.

reaches down to help Jamal get up

Come on we have to g…

Screams of pain comes from Tracey

Jamal: WHAT THE FUCK IS WRON…

Jamal looks down to see a wolf has its teeth biting into Tracy's ankle. The wolf then begins to try and drag her to the ground and back to its pack.

Tracey: *Trying to kick at the wolf loses her balance and falls*

Jamal, help me!

Jamal: *Looks at Tracey*

Good luck.

Tries to run away while struggling to breath.

Tracey: *Screams*

NOOOOOOO!

*Tries to grab onto anything she can and kicks at the wolf's face, but his teeth are deep into her ankle and he is not letting go. *

Jamal: *slowly making his way to the cabin*

Okay, not much further now, I see the cabin.

Lisa: *Sees Jamal and runs to him*

Where is Tracey?

Jamal: *coughs*

Not sure, I thought she was with you guys in front of me.

Lisa: *realization sets in Lisa's face*

 Oh no…

Lisa runs back to the main road hoping and praying she doesn't find her friend Tracey dead.

Wolves are growling and fighting over Tracey's body

Lisa: Oh my God… Tracey no.

Blinded by rage Lisa finds a large stick and quietly walks up to the wolf chewing on Tracey's femur and WHACK! The wolf yelps and then growls and turns to see what just hit him to see Lisa there not frozen in fear as the wolf raises up and swings his paw at Lisa slashing her shoulder open sending a red mist into the air and sending Lisa falling onto her back and snapping the drunk rage she was in

I am going to die…

Growling grows closer as Lisa lays there on the ground waiting for the finally blow to join her friends Tracey and LJ

Chris: *Yells*

OVER HERE, YOU FLEA BITTEN !

GUN FIRE ERUPTS

Patty: *Grabs Lisa and yells*

I GOT HER! CHRIS COME ON!

Chris: *YELLS*

OKAY, ELLIOTT, GIVE COVER FIRE!

Park Ranger Elliott: *YELLS*

ON IT!

*Starts shooting. The wolves ran away all except one wolf stayed still and stood on his hind legs staring at Park Ranger Elliott as he shot and when Elliott notches him and shot at him and then the wolf ran off with the rest of the pack. The three make it back to the cabin where the remaining friends and Park Ranger were.

CHAPTER 11
THE END IS NEAR

Chris: Where are the medical supplies?

Park Ranger Stacey: Over here!

grabs med kit

Here, here are some bandages and what of the painkillers we have left in here.

Jamal: I'll need someone to check me out, too.

Chris: Man, not now. Lisa is losing a lot of blood; we have to slow or stop the bleeding somehow! This cut is deep but can be closed doesn't look like it hit anything major.

Patty: Where is the cut?

Park Ranger Elliott: It is across her chest

Chris: Hey Patty, come here and apply pressure to this towel. I have an idea, and she's not going to like it. Hey look, I need a knife and something that can heat up!

Ranger Stacey: For what?

Chris: I am going to close the cut to stop the bleeding and hopefully give us enough time to get help.

Patty: Are you sure about that?

Jamal: Bro, the smell of burning flesh would bring those things to us, use your head, damn!

Park Ranger Stacey: I hate to say it, but Jamal has a point.

Lisa: *groans*

Do it…

Patty: What?

Lisa: Do it, and pour water over it and then whatever happens happens, but we need to get out of here before they come here and get us!

Chris: Are you sure?

Lisa: Yeah, just give me something to bite down on.

Chris: Okay, we'll find something, and we'll get the knife going.

Lisa: Okay.

Jamal: Are you people crazy?! This will get us all killed!

Park Ranger Stacey: So what is your bright idea?

Jamal: I don't know but not fucking this shit!

Patty: If you do not have an idea than shut the fuck up!

Chris: Man chill the hell out damn! We're all trying to survive here!

Jamal: Yeah

Chris: Okay, looks like the knife is ready. Patty, are you ready?

Lisa: Ready as I'll ever be…

Chris: Okay, listen everyone, this smell will be very bad and Patty it will hurt here is a damped rag to bite.

Lisa takes deep breaths and tries to take her mind to a different place

Chris: Everyone hold her down.

Chris places the burning red blade on Lisa's wound sizzling

Lisa screams and bites the rag then starts shaking

Patty: Why is she doing that?

Park Ranger Elliott: She's going into shock!

Chris: Okay, okay almost and done.

Lisa: *Heavily breathing*

That… That um wasn't so bad.

passes out

Patty: Chris, is she going to be okay?

Chris: Yeah hopefully, her body just went through a lot. Let her sleep for a bit and then we're going to head to the roads.

Park Ranger Elliott: Look, Stacey and I are going to stay behind and hold them things off when they come.

Chris: Why would you stay and not come?

Park Ranger Stacey: I am injured and can hardly walk let alone run. And I've lost too much blood from my wounds. So I will stay here, let them smell my blood and come to me, and my rifle will teach them how to keep their claws to themselves. And I refuse to die and not take one out for taking out Lucky…

Patty: *Holding Lisa's head rubbing it*

Hey Lisa, you need to wake up, we're getting ready to leave.

Lisa: *groans*

I was having such a good nap.

tries to stand up and gets dizzy

Chris: Aye take it easy.

Lisa: I'm… ugh I'm okay ready to leave and take a hot shower.

Chris: Are you su…?

Jamal: *interrupts Chris*

Look man, she said she's fine! Lets gg…

A very loud howl can be heard, a howl so loud and vicious that it shook the cabin and made everyone's bones weak.

Jamal: Wwwhat… What the hell was that!

Park Ranger Elliott: I'm not a zoologist, but I'd think that was the alpha.

Patty: The what?

Chris: The alpha, leader of the pack. And he sounds pissed.

The howl can be heard again only this time seemed more vicious

Jamal: We have to leave now!

Park Ranger Elliott: He's right, leave now and we'll do what we can to hold them back for you guys to escape.

Patty: *Helping Lisa walk to the door*

Hey Elliott and Stacey, ya don't have to do this.

Park Ranger Stacey: If saving you guys cost us our lives, it was worth it.

Chris: Alright, come everyone let's move.

Opens and holds the door for Jamal, Patty & Lisa to leave. Looking back at the park rangers loading up the rest of the ammo they have left.

One last time, are you guys sure?

Park Rangers: Yeah.

Park Ranger Stacey: Chris be careful of Jamal, someone that is scared will do anything to survive. I'll watch him but he's just scared is all. And here take this flare you only have one shot, use it wisely.

Patty: Chris come on!

Chris: Thank you fellas again and I will, and good luck!

Park Ranger Stacey: Same to you.

Door closes and footsteps heard heading away from the cabin

Park Ranger Elliott: *Goes and locks the door*

Hey, Stacey.

Park Ranger Stacey: Yo?

Park Ranger Elliott: Do you think they'll make it?

Park Ranger Stacey: Honestly, I don't think so especially with Jamal freaking out and the knife burn girl possibly still bleeding on the inside. There is a chance they can make it but who knows.

Park Ranger Elliott: Hopefully the call for help we made comes in time.

Howls right outside of the cabin, louder now that the wolves are right there.

Park Ranger Elliott: *Looks out the window*

Holy shit, there and I see so many red eyes…

Dripping noise can be heard coming from where Elliott was standing

Park Ranger Stacey: Bro, did you just…

Park Ranger Elliott: The alpha is he…

The cabin door gets kicked in and next thing you hear is gun fire and a lot of cursing!

Patty: Oh my God, do you hear that…

Jamal: No shit, we hear that shit, we need to hurry up and get out these woods!

Chris: Jamal cut the smart as remarks we need to work together in order to survive this shit!

Lisa: Hey guys.

Patty: Yeah, honey?

Lisa: I don't feel so good…

Chris: What do you mean?

Lisa: I feel dizzy kind of.

Patty: Yeah, she's burning up.

Jamal: I told ya not to do that knife shit to her. She may be bleeding on the inside and can get infected.

Chris: Okay, let's pick up the pace and hurry to the main road.

Patty: Okay, come on Lisa.

Jamal: *Looking behind him and notices red eyes but does not say anything except for…* Okay, let's go.

But he stays near Lisa and Patty. Jamal thinks, "If those wolves catch up, one of these girls will have to be used for a distraction so I can get away. I refuse to die out here. I have more to live for."

Chris: Aye Jamal.

Jamal: *snaps out of his own thoughts*

Yeah, what's up?

Chris: We're going to have to protect the girls, especially Lisa, she isn't looking so good.

Jamal: Man, what? And what about us?

Chris: Bro, what about us?

Jamal: I do not want to die!

Chris: And we won't as long as we keep moving and work together!

Jamal: Okay... Yeah, it's only the four of us left, and you're right Chris if we work together we can survive this.

Patty: Hey guys, do you hear that?

Helicopter noises circling around the area

Chris: Yeah, I do.

Jamal: Holy shit, we're saved! We're sa... they're flying away!

Patty: How are we going to get their attention?

Chris: I have an idea, but we need to move fast!

Patty: What about Lisa? And those wolves behind us?

Chris: You're right, it's been quiet for a while, and I have no idea what they can be up to right now. So listen here is the plan... Patty and Lisa, you two continue walking the main road. I will jog up and shoot the flare the park rangers gave me to get the pilots attention to come back. Jamal, listen, you stay with the girls to help Patty carry Lisa.

Jamal: And what if the wolves come?!

Chris: *Pulls out a knife*

It is not much but take this. ***hands it to Jamal***

Jamal: *Takes knife*

Why don't I run and try to catch the helicopter and you stay with the girls?

Chris: Because I am faster than you and more conditioned. Look man, we do not have time for this. I will be back before anything will happen.

Jamal: Okay, man, just hurry up then.

Patty: Yes, please hurry back, Chris.

Lisa: I believe in you, Chris.

Chrishears the fear in Patty's voice and knows he should've stayed but knew he was the best option to get help for his friends and himself

CHAPTER 12
SAVED OR ARE YOU MISTAKEN?

Jamal: Hey Patty, how is Lisa doing?

Patty: She's doing okay, I think her body is on autopilot.

Jamal: What do you mean?

Patty: Like she is walking leaning on me but she's not talking, and her breathing is like normal but not normal in a way like it's hard to explain to be honest.

Jamal: Yeah, I got you.

Howling can be heard in the distance

Patty: Oh shit, oh shit. Jamal, did you hear that?

Jamal: Fuck fuck!

Lisa: W…what's going on?

Jamal: Shut the hell up, Lisa, or they'll hear you…

Patty: Jamal, relax! They'll hear you before they hear her.

Jamal: Listen if they get any closer to us then it is every man for themselves.

Patty: *shocked look on her face*

What the hell is that supposed to mean?

Jamal: Don't play dumb right now!

Lisa: What is going on?

Patty: Lisa, honey, I need you to stay quiet, okay?

Lisa: I just want to know what is going on and why there's red eyes looking at us?

Both Jamal & Patty look at Lisa

Jamal: Fucking what is looking at us?!

Growling can be heard in the bushes just ahead of Lisa, Patty & Jamal.

Jamal: Fuck!

Patty: Stand still… no one moves!

Jamal: The fuck this isn't a damn T- rex it can see us!

Patty: I get that but why hasn't it attacked yet? I think it may be scared because he knows we outnumber him.

Jamal: You have a point.

Lisa: *Throws up blood*

Guys, I do not feel so good.

Patty: Shit, she does have a cut. She is bleeding from within her body!

Jamal: See, I told ya dumbasses not to do that dumb shit with the knife!

And as if things couldn't get any worse there it is again the howl that would shake a mountain down to rumble

Jamal: I… I don't want to die here!

Patty: And we won't let us keep mo…

Jamal: *Runs off in the direction Chris went*

EVERY MAN FOR THEMSELVES!

Patty: What the fuc...

Lisa: *Screams*

SHIT!

Patty: What?!? What is i…

Lisa's body is pulled away from Patty sending her to the ground and Lisa is dragged by a wolf into the brush. There is growling and snarling.

Patty: Lisa!!! NO!!

Chris: *Hears the screams***

Dear God, please keep them alive. I need to find a clearing or something for them to land, but they're getting too fa,r fuck it!

Loads a flare and shoots in the sky

Please see it, come on come on...

Helicopter continues to fly away

FUCK,SHIT, Fu…

Helicopter noise can be heard flying back

Yes, they saw the flare I have to get the others!

Jamal: Fuck, how far did Chris run to man, damn.

Howling from the wolves and then rain starts to come down

Jamal: Oh great…

Lisa: *screaming in pain for help*

PATTTTY HELP ME!

Patty: *Without thinking runs to Lisa's aid only to encounter the same fate as her, with a wolf biting arm as she reached for Lisa and she screams and then whispers*

I'll see you soon LJ…

Then the wolf upcuts Patty with his razor-sharp paws killing her

Chris: *Running to the last place he saw his three remaining friends alive*

Where are they?! I couldn't have gone that far?

Chris hears footsteps coming towards fast and runs towards the steps hoping for the best WHO IS THAT?! It can only be two things: a friend or death… WHO IS IT?!

Jamal: *Yells*

CHRIS???

Chris: Jamal? Thank God! Jamal…

Jamal: We have to leave now!

Chris: I know. Where the girls are?

Jamal: What do you mean, where are the girls? Where is the helicopter going to pick us up?

Chris: I'm not sure, but we'll have to find a spot. But where are the girls?

Jamal: *sighs*

I don't know…

Chris: *Punches Jamal in the face* What do you mean, you don't know? I left them in your care to keep them safe and you left them!

Jamal: *Getting back up* Did you hit me for saving my ass over dying for those bitches? ***Throws left hook***

Chris: *Dodges the hook and counters with jab and Jamal falls back on his ass*

The fuck is wrong with you man the hell up and protect someone else other than your damn self!

Jamal: *laying on his back, slowly getting up*

Okay, okay, no more. I'm sorry, you're right. I was scared to die, and I dropped the knife when I heard the howls and while I was running away.

Chris: So those screams I heard were…

Jamal: *sighs*

Yeah, Patty and Lisa are dead…

Chris: *Falls to his knees*

FUCK!

Helicopter noise slowly approaching

Jamal: *Getting up slowly*

Do you hear that?

Chris: Yeah, I d…

The split second of happiness was short-lived when the howling of multiple wolves can be heard

Jamal: What the fuck… damn… Chris, how many flares do you have left?

Chris: I have two left… Jamal, look out!

Jamal jumps out the way right before a wolf bites him, and Chris shoots a flare directly into the wolf's mouth sending him back into the brush

Chris: *rushes over to help up Jamal* Nice dive!

Jamal: Good sh…

The earth shocking howl from the alpha can be heard once again

Jamal: See the fuck you done did, man! We have to run towards the helicopter and hope for the best!

Chris: You're right let's go!

The two renaming friends start running towards the helicopter noise hoping they'll provide safety

The noise is increasing loud and louder of the helicopter blades slicing into the night almost morning sky

Chris: We must be getting close, they're getting louder!

Jamal: Good, because my lungs and legs cannot keep running much longer. Remind me to get a gym membership once we get back!

Chris: Sure thing.

Howling of the alpha can be heard closing in on the two

Jamal: This thing will not give up!

Chris: Look we're close enough, hold on I'm going to shoot the last flare.

Jamal: Okay.

Chris: *Shoots the last flare*

Come on, please see it.

Helicopter pilot: *Over the Helicopters mega phone*

We see the flare. Please stay where you are, we are coming to get you!

As the flare is coming down something they did not want to see is standing in the tree line looking at them with eyes redder than the devil, taller than any human man could be and it steps towards Chris and Jamal showing his long sharp teeth.

Helicopter pilot: *announces* There are too many trees for me to land. There is a clearing a hundred fifty yards in the direction you're both facing. I'll meet you both there.

The pilot starts heading towards the location

Jamal: Shit... shit what are we going today?

Chris: Simple… we charge that bitch. I'll throw the flare gun at his face to cause him to be distracted and we just run to the helicopter and tell him to take off face as much as possible!

Jamal: Um yeah, sure okay.

Little did Chris know Jamal had his own plan. A plan that he would not see the next morning.

FINAL CHAPTER
MISSING PERSONS

Chris: On three we run!

Jamal: Okay.

Chris: *Begins to count*

One…two... three… GO!

*Both men run right at the wolf, and Chris does what he said by throwing the flare gun at the wolf's face. *

Whack

Direct hit in the wolf's nose confusing the elf and also angering the wolf at the same time but giving them the time to get to the clearing.

Wolf howling in pain

Chris: We're almost…

yells in pain

Jamal, I think he got me…

Jamal: *Running past Chris beginning to drag himself along the dirt*

Yells I'm sorry I have to live, I don't want to die!

Chris: *Yells as he's pulling out the knife from the back of his thigh. Begins to pull himself up on a tree to hop towards the helicopter.*

FUCK YOU!

Jamal: *Hauling ass* I'm sorry!

Bursts through the bushes to the helicopter and runs to board

Helicopter Pilot: Where are the Rangers they found for help?

Jamal: They're dead, we need to leave now!

Helicopter Pilot: Where's your friend? There were two of you, right?

Jamal: Yeah, something chasing is grabbed hi…

Helicopter Pilot: There he is, right there. He looks seriously hurt. Go help him.

Chris: Help me!

Jamal: Look, get us in the air now!

Chris: *Wolf from the bushes grabs Chris and he yells*

AHHHHHHH!

Helicopter Pilot: WHAT THE HELL IS THAT!?!?

Jamal: GO NOW!

Helicopter Pilot: *Starts Pulling the Helicopter up*

Jesus, buckle up!

Jamal: *Sits down and buckles up*

Okay, I'm in. Let's go, let's go!

Just as soon as the helicopter is flying away a loud BOOM is heard and emergency sirens and lights flashing

Helicopter Pilot: SHIT, SHIT, WE'RE GOING DOWN!

*** Jamal and the pilot both YELL***

AHHHHHHHHHH!

Helicopter crashes, Fire crackling, the wolf howls and slowly walks into the dark forest as the sun rises

News Anchor: Hello my name is Katy Bonds. Today on channel 1 Tender Love, and yes, we care news the search for the remains of the six friends Luis, Tracey, Lisa, Patty, Chris, and Jamal along with the National Park rangers and the helicopter pilot Bruce. Family members of the friends say they went on a camping trip in Flathead National Forest. The authorities are still waiting for the black box from the crashed helicopter to see what was going on before the crash. We'll have more at 9 P.M. thank you, and remember to be tender love and care. I'm Katy Bonds see you later, Montana.